THE DIAMOND TREE
Jewish Tales from Around the World

The Diamond Tree

Jewish Tales from Around the World

SELECTED AND RETOLD
BY HOWARD SCHWARTZ
AND BARBARA RUSH

ILLUSTRATED BY
URI SHULEVITZ

HarperCollins*Publishers*

The artwork for this book was
done in watercolor.

The Diamond Tree: Jewish Tales from Around the World
Text copyright © 1991 by Howard Schwartz and Barbara Rush
Illustrations copyright © 1991 by Uri Shulevitz ,
Printed in the U.S.A. All rights reserved.
Typography by Al Cetta
1 2 3 4 5 6 7 8 9 10
First Edition

Library of Congress Cataloging-in-Publication Data
Schwartz, Howard, date
   The diamond tree : Jewish tales from around the world /
selected and retold by Howard Schwartz and Barbara Rush ;
illustrated by Uri Shulevitz.
         p.   cm.
   Summary: A collection of traditional Jewish tales from many
different countries.
   ISBN 0-06-025239-1. — ISBN 0-06-025243-X (lib. bdg.)
   1. Legends, Jewish—Juvenile literature.   [1. Folklore, Jewish.]
I. Rush, Barbara.   II. Shulevitz, Uri, date, ill.   III. Title.
PZ8.1.S4Di 1991   90-32420
398.2′089′924—dc20   CIP
                                                            AC

"The Magic Pitcher" and "The Prince Who Thought He Was a
Rooster" first appeared in *Cricket* magazine.

Ask now the beasts, and they shall teach you,
And the birds of the air, and they shall tell you,
Or speak to the earth, and it shall teach you,
And the fishes of the sea shall instruct you.

Job 12:7–8

CONTENTS

INTRODUCTION

FOLKTALES are the first stories a child is told. They address a child's most basic concerns and impart morals, and though they are sometimes frightening, they almost always have happy endings.

Every culture has its own folktales. Some of these are variants of old, familiar stories, and can be found in many different cultures. Since the Jewish people have lived all over the world, versions of many familiar stories are found with a Jewish element added—for example, the king in the story becomes King Solomon, or the giant is the biblical giant Og. In this collection, Og becomes part of the story of Noah's ark.

There are also tales unique to Jewish culture—they cannot be found anywhere else. "Chusham and the Wind" is an example of this type of story. Chusham, a uniquely Jewish character, is a foolish but lovable boy, known to Jewish children throughout Eastern Europe and the Middle East.

Whether unique or universal, each of the stories in this book concerns a fundamental teaching of Judaism, such as honesty, faith, charity, or cooperation. Other, more pragmatic lessons may also be taught—in "The Bear and the Children," children learn never to open the door to strangers.

All the tales included here are drawn from authentic Jewish sources, both ancient and modern, from all over the world. These sources include the Talmud, the Midrash, the earliest Jewish folk anthology (*The Alphabet of Ben Sira*), Hasidic lore, Eastern European folklore, and Middle Eastern folklore. Several of the stories have been selected from the Israel Folktale Archives, which has collected stories from every Jewish ethnic group in Israel.

Whatever the source, many of these stories survived for centuries in the oral tradition before being written down. In virtually every case they were told, rather than read, by parents to their children, who, in turn, told them to *their* children, and so on down through the generations.

The very diversity of the sources for these tales testifies to the long and scattered history of the Jewish people and the many countries through which they have wandered. But the tales not only reflect the culture of the region in which they originated; they also remain true to the Jewish tradition that keeps them alive.

THE GIANT OG AND THE ARK

Long, LONG AGO—as long ago as anyone can remember—there were many giants in the world. Then God sent the great flood, and when the waters rose as high as the tops of mountains, even higher than the tallest giant, there was only one giant on earth who did not drown.

This giant's name was Og, and it was he who helped Noah collect one pair of every kind of animal to bring into the ark. Og went to the four corners of the earth, from the coldest to the hottest, from the darkest to the brightest, and he found every animal on earth, as Noah asked him to do. He brought the elephant, the kangaroo, and the giraffe. He brought the camel, the zebra, and the monkey. And it did not take Og very long, because every step he took was three miles long.

Soon the animals were safe inside the ark. The great rains began to fall and the waters began to rise. Noah was

[13]

just about to set sail when Og came to him and begged, "Please, Noah, don't leave me here to drown. Let me come along too."

"Very well," said Noah. "You have been a good helper, and you deserve to be saved. But how will you fit inside the ark?"

"Let me sit on the roof," Og said.

Noah was afraid. What if the great weight of the giant sinks the ark? he thought. But Og climbed onto the roof and sat there, and the ark did not sink. Then Noah knew that God wanted him to save the giant. The rain fell on Og and he was drenched to the bone. And he shivered and shook, great giant though he was.

On the third day, when the ark was out in the middle of the sea, Og realized that he was hungry, for he had not had a single thing to eat since setting sail. He knocked on the roof, and the ark rolled from side to side. Noah climbed up to the rafters. "What do you want?" he shouted.

"I'm hungry!" Og roared back.

"What do you like to eat?" asked Noah, who had found out the right thing to feed each animal on the ark but had not had time to think of what giants eat.

"I eat trees," Og roared back. Now Noah looked around, and there was not a single tree to be seen. What am I going to do with a starving giant on the roof? he wondered. "There aren't any trees," he called back.

[14]

"In that case," Og thundered, "do you have any leaves?"

"Yes, yes, we have lots of leaves," said Noah, for one corner of the ark was filled with leaves to feed the giraffes. "How many do you eat?"

"One thousand buckets a day!" Og answered.

Noah gulped. How could he find so many leaves? Then the giraffes, who had overheard the giant's request, came to Noah. "We will share our leaves with the giant Og, for after all, it was he who brought us safely to the ark."

And the turtles stuck their heads out of their shells. "We will share our leaves too," they said, "for it was Og who brought us safely to the ark."

Finally the caterpillars spoke. "We will share our leaves too, for after all, Og brought us to the ark."

Noah was pleased. But now he had a new problem. How could he pass the food to the giant without going outside the ark? This time the giant himself had a solution. Og put his pinky into the roof of the ark and made a hole. Then he covered the hole with his hand to keep the rain from pouring into the ark.

Then all the animals came forth and made a chain. The ant passed the leaves to the mouse; the mouse, to the turtle; the turtle, to the rabbit; the rabbit, to the monkey; the monkey, to the elephant; the elephant, to the giraffe— who stretched and stretched and stretched his long neck until he reached the roof and passed the leaves to the hungry giant. And Og swallowed them all in a single gulp.

But just as the animals were starting to settle down, they heard the giant's knock again. The ark shook. Noah climbed back up to the rafters. "What do you want?" he shouted.

"I'm thirsty," Og roared back.

"What do you like to drink?" called Noah.

"I drink milk," roared the giant.

"How much do you drink?" asked Noah.

"A thousand cups a day!" roared the giant.

Noah gasped. "Oh, dear, how will we find that much milk?"

He quickly got an answer "*Moo! Moo!* Give our milk to Og," the cows said, "for he was the one who brought us here safely."

The camels, who had been listening, came to join the cows. "We will give our milk as well," they said, "for it was the giant Og who brought us here."

And the goats came to join the camels. "*Meh! Meh!* We want to share our milk too," they offered, "for the giant Og brought us safely to the ark."

So once again the animals formed a chain: the ant, the mouse, the turtle, the rabbit, the monkey, the elephant, and at last the tall giraffe, until all the milk was passed through the hole to the thirsty giant. And Og gulped it down in a single swallow.

The animals had just gone back to their places, when once again there was a knock on the roof. The ark shook from side to side. Noah climbed to the rafters. "What do you want now?"

"It's hard to sit up here," roared the giant. "I need a pillow!"

Poor Noah! What was he to do? Where could he find a pillow for the giant Og? But he didn't have to worry long, for suddenly all the birds of the ark—peacocks and eagles, hummingbirds and canaries, big birds and small ones—flew toward him. "We will share our feathers," they chirped. Soon there were feathers of all sizes, all colors, all shapes, piled up as high as the roof. Noah and his wife and sons sewed one hundred sheets together and made a giant-sized pillow case, and all the animals helped them stuff it with the feathers. Then Noah called the strong gorilla to squeeze the pillow through the hole.

Just then, the snake slithered up. "All the animals have been helping. I want to help too," he said. "Here, take my skin. It will make a raincoat for the giant." And so the snakeskin was passed up too.

Now, up on the roof, the giant Og was no longer hungry. He was no longer thirsty. He had a soft pillow to sit on. And he had a raincoat to keep him dry. Oh, he was happy! He was so happy that he began to sing.

[19]

And as he sang, the ark rocked from side to side. But the animals inside did not complain, for they were happy too, knowing that they had helped their friend who, after all, had saved them. For the rest of the forty days and forty nights, Og sat on his pillow on the roof and sang. And his friends below danced around in a ring, and as they danced, they sang with him:

"Og is sitting on the roof.
Og is sitting on the roof.
He's as happy as can be.
He's so happy. So are we!"

PALESTINE: c. EIGHTH CENTURY

THE MAGIC PITCHER

LONG AGO, in the land of Iraq, there lived a potter who was very poor. He worked hard from morning till night, making pots and pitchers, but even so, he barely earned enough to feed his family. This potter had a young daughter whose name was Rachel. She loved to watch her father work, for she, too, liked to mold the soft clay.

One day the potter showed his daughter how to use the wheel on which he made his pots. He let her cast one by herself, and she shaped it like a vase. Next she added a handle to make the vase into a pitcher.

Oh, what a beautiful pitcher it was—small and round and perfectly formed. Rachel painted lovely flowers on it and decorated the handle with olive leaves. Then she held it in her hands and looked inside. To her surprise, she saw a little puddle of olive oil at the bottom! And as she watched, the oil rose slowly in the pitcher.

"Father, Father," she called. "Come see!"

Her father came running. "It's a miracle," he cried. He sniffed the precious oil and watched it rise, as if by magic.

The pitcher filled itself with oil to the very rim—and then stopped. Rachel and her father dipped their fingers into the oil and tasted it. Much to their delight, they discovered that it was the finest oil they had ever had.

"How I wish we could give this oil to your grandmother," the potter said. "She hasn't had any for many months."

"Oh, Father, let me take it to her," Rachel said.

Her father was happy that Rachel was so unselfish, but he answered, "No, Rachel, it is too far to Grandmother's house, and you are too young to go by yourself." But Rachel begged and pleaded and promised she would be careful, and at last her father agreed to let her go.

The potter hitched their only donkey to a wooden cart. He carefully loaded the pitcher filled with olive oil, and then added four jugs, each closed with a cork. Rachel was to take these to Grandmother, too. One jug was filled with milk, another with honey, one with wine, and one with vinegar. The potter placed them around the pitcher to keep the oil from spilling. Finally Rachel kissed her father good-bye and set out on the long road to Grandmother's house.

Rachel drove the cart very slowly so the pitcher would

not be shaken. But soon the cart went over a little bump in the road, and some of the olive oil spilled out.

Oh, dear, Rachel thought, how will I ever get this oil to Grandmother's house without spilling it?

Just then she heard a scratchy voice from somewhere inside the wagon. "Rachel, the road to your grandmother's house is very long. I can get you there in a wink, but you must give me all of your oil."

Now, Rachel was not the least bit frightened when she heard that voice. In fact, she was angry—and even though she didn't know to whom she was speaking, she said, "What good would it do if I arrived without the oil? No, thank you. I will get to Grandmother's by myself."

There was no answer. Rachel drove on. But she had gone only a little farther down the road when she passed over another bump, and a little more of the oil spilled out.

As Rachel was wondering what to do, the scratchy voice piped up again, "Rachel, I can get you to Grandmother's in a wink, but you must give me all of your oil."

Again Rachel said, "No, thank you, I will get there by myself." And on she drove.

She had gone only a little farther down the road when the cart struck a huge bump and almost tipped over. Nearly all the oil spilled out. Rachel felt like crying. What was she to do now? Again the voice spoke up, "Rachel, I can get you to Grandmother's in a wink, but you must give me all of your oil."

By this time Rachel knew that the voice was coming from one of the jugs, and she became furious. "Where are you, you evil thing? It was *you* who caused the oil to spill!" She began to pull the corks out of the jugs. There was nothing odd in the jug of milk, nor in the jug of honey, nor in the jug of wine. But when she pulled the cork out of the last jug, the one filled with vinegar, *poof!* Rachel suddenly found herself sitting in front of her grandmother's house.

"H-h-how did I get here?" Rachel asked aloud. And from behind her a scratchy voice answered, "Rachel, it was I who brought you here."

Rachel quickly turned around. A little man, no bigger than one of the jugs, was sitting on the floor of the cart. His pants and shirt were baggy. There was a stocking cap on his head and a pipe hanging out of his mouth—and he looked very annoyed indeed.

"I am the imp who was hiding in the jug of vinegar," he said. "By pulling out the cork, you forced me to bring you here as quick as a wink, even though you never promised me the oil." He stamped his foot in anger. "That oil should be *mine!*" he cried. Then he vanished into thin air.

Relieved that the imp was gone, Rachel jumped down from the cart and hurried to the door. "Grandmother,

Grandmother," she called, "see what I have brought you." Grandmother and Rachel kissed and hugged each other with joy. Then Rachel brought the jugs into the house, one at a time. How pleased Grandmother was to see one jug filled with milk, one with honey, one with wine, and one with vinegar.

Rachel returned to the cart to get her own beautiful pitcher. When she looked inside and saw that only a single drop of oil was left, she began to cry. But as she picked the pitcher up in her hands, it began to fill again, just as it had the first time. Lo and behold, the oil kept rising until the pitcher was completely full.

"What miracle is this?" cried Grandmother. "Rachel, my child, tell me what happened."

So Rachel told her grandmother about the pitcher she had made and how it had miraculously filled with oil, and about the journey to her grandmother's house and the voice from the jug and the little man who smoked a pipe.

Her grandmother nodded wisely. "Rachel," she said, "you have been blessed with a magic pitcher. If you had accepted the imp's offer, the pitcher would have lost its magic powers. Now it will always fill again, whenever you hold it in your hands."

And that is exactly what happened. Rachel poured that wonderful olive oil into every empty jug in her grandmother's house. Together they put the jugs into the

[27]

cart and took them to the village to sell. This time Rachel's cart did not hit a single bump, nor did she spill a single drop of oil. Soon there were enough gold coins to buy Grandmother everything she would need for a long, long time.

From then on, the magic pitcher supplied all the olive oil Rachel could ever use. Whenever she wished for more, she simply held the pitcher in her hands.

And so it was that Rachel and her family were never poor again—and they gladly shared the wealth from their magic pitcher with all those who were in need.

IRAQ: ORAL TRADITION

CHUSHAM AND THE WIND

CHUSHAM was a little boy who lived in Iraq. He liked to go to the market to buy things for his mother. But sometimes by the time he got there, he couldn't remember exactly what he was supposed to do.

Once there was going to be a big party at Chusham's house, because Chusham's sister was going to get married very soon. Chusham's mother wanted to cook chickens and bake cakes and cook other good foods for the wedding party, so she sent Chusham to the market.

"Chusham," she said, "buy two chickens and get them home as fast as you can."

"Yes, Mother," said Chusham—and off he went.

At the market, Chusham bought two big plump chickens, which were strutting about happily, showing off their strong wings.

"Oh, these chickens have such strong wings," said Chusham. "Surely they can fly home quicker than I can walk." He pointed the chickens in the direction of his house. "Fly straight to my house," he told them, and then he walked home by himself.

When Chusham got home, there were no chickens. "Where are the chickens?" asked Chusham's mother. And Chusham told her what he had done.

"My dear Chusham," said his mother, "chickens cannot find their way home by themselves. Chickens must be tied together by their feet. You must carry them carefully, and when you get home, they will be safe."

"Yes, Mother," said Chusham.

The next day Chusham's mother sent him to the market to buy fifty eggs. "This time I will remember what to do," said Chusham, and he tied the eggs together, one by one. Then he lifted the string high in the air and ran home.

When he got there, the eggs were broken. Gooey egg whites and sticky egg yolks were streaming all over the street. "Oh, Chusham, what happened?" asked his father. And Chusham told him what he had done.

"Eggs," said Chusham's father, "must not be tied together with a string. Eggs must be put into a basket filled with straw. Then when you get home, they will not be broken."

"Yes, Father," said Chusham.

The next day Chusham's mother sent him to the market to buy a fresh fish. Chusham bought the biggest fish he could carry. This time I will remember what to do, he thought, and he put the fish in a basket filled with straw. Then he went home.

But when he got there, the fish was dead. "Chusham, what happened to the fish?" asked his sister. Chusham told her what he had done.

"Oh, Chusham, a fish does not belong in a basket," she said. "A fish must be put into a bowl of water. You must carry it oh, so carefully. Then when you get home, it will not be dead."

"Yes, dear Sister," said Chusham.

The next day Chusham's mother sent him to the market to buy some oil. Chusham ran happily all the way. This time I will remember what to do, he thought.

Chusham bought a big jug of oil and poured it into a bowl of water. He lifted it up oh, so carefully, and, holding it in his hands, tiptoed all the way home. But when he got there, the oil was spoiled.

"Chusham, what happened to the oil?" asked his brother. Chusham told him what he had done.

"Dear Chusham," said his brother, "oil must not be put into a bowl of water. Oil must be poured into a can. Then when you get home, it will not be spoiled."

KATANYA

ONCE UPON A TIME there was a poor old woman. All her life she had wished for a child of her own. But though she wished and wished, she never had any children.

Her husband died, and still she wanted a child. "Oh, how wonderful it would be if only I had a little boy or girl," she said. So she prayed to God to help her.

God saw how lonely the old woman was and sent Elijah to visit her. Elijah is a prophet who often returns to earth in the form of an old man to help his people, the Jews, when they are in trouble. But no one knows who he is. Sometimes he disguises himself as a beggar, and sometimes he dresses like a merchant. And sometimes he uses the powers of God to work his magic.

Now this old woman had worked hard all of her life, but she had no money left and nothing to sell for food. So each day she went to the market to ask the merchants for what they could spare: one peach, one apricot, one little olive. Sometimes they took pity on her and gave her a piece of fruit. And some days that was all she had to eat.

But one day all the merchants were in a bad mood because the king had raised their taxes. And when the old woman begged for fruit, each and every one of them shooed her away. She did not get anything—not one peach, not one apricot, not one little olive. The old woman was very sad, for it looked as if she would go hungry all day long.

Just as she was about to leave the market, she noticed a merchant she had never seen before, an old man who looked as poor as she was. As she walked over to the old man, she saw that all he had left were six brown dates, drying in the sun.

"Could you spare just one?" she asked.

"Surely," said the old man (who was really Elijah). "Take the one you want."

Now five of the dates were very little, but one was big, and that is the one she chose. "Thank you, kind sir," she said, and went on her way.

When she got home, the old woman placed the date on the windowsill, where sunlight shone on it. "You know," the old woman said to herself, "this is such a beautiful date, I don't have the heart to eat it." So she left it there, even though she was hungry, and went out to see if she

could find something else to eat.

The sun continued to shine on the date until it was quite warm. Soon the date began to stir, as if something were inside. All at once it broke open—and out popped a little girl. She was no bigger than a little finger, and she wore a pretty dress of many colors. The little girl stood up on the windowsill and looked around. The house was quite bare—only a bed and a table and a chair stood in the room—and it wasn't very clean, for the old woman's broom had only a few straws left.

The first thing the little girl did was to climb out the window. She saw a ball of string hanging on the wall and, grabbing one end of the string, she lowered herself down to the ground. There she picked some of the short grasses, because she was very short herself, and she tied the bundle together with another piece of straw. "Oh, what a perfect broom for me!" she cried.

Back up the string and onto the windowsill she climbed, and then she started to clean the house. She swept from corner to corner, until the floor sparkled like new.

Meanwhile, the old woman was still walking on the road, searching for some food, when whom should she meet but the old man who had given her the date! The old man smiled and this time he gave her a large shiny olive. She thanked him and he continued on his way. When the old woman bit into the olive, what did she find inside but a golden coin! She hurried after the old man to give it back, but he was nowhere to be found. The golden coin was hers to keep. What a lucky day for me! she thought.

But she was even more surprised when she got home, for there was her house, all neat and clean! She couldn't believe her eyes. "Who did this?" she asked out loud.

"I did, Mother," said a tiny voice.

The old woman looked around. There on the windowsill, where the old woman had left the date, was the tiniest girl in the world, a girl no bigger than the woman's little finger. The old woman blinked to see if she was dreaming. "Did you call me Mother?"

"Yes, Mother," said the girl. And at that moment the old woman realized that the kind old man must have been Elijah the prophet. And she hugged the tiny girl very carefully, so as not to hurt her.

Then she asked the girl her name. But the girl did not answer. "No one has given me a name," she said at last.

"Then I will name you!" said the old woman. She thought and thought. "I will call you Katanya, the little one," she said. And so it was that her name became Katanya.

Katanya and the old woman lived together happily in that little hut. With the help of the golden coin they never had to go hungry. And the first thing the old woman did with the money was to pay back every merchant who had given her fruit to eat.

The old woman loved Katanya with all her heart. She made a little bed for her inside a teacup. She fashioned a fur hat for her from a bunny's tail, shoes out of tiny nutshells, and dresses made of rose petals. But of all her clothes, Katanya loved best her dress of many colors, the one she had been wearing when she first popped out of the date.

Katanya helped her mother by sweeping out the house with her tiny broom. She even cleaned between the boards of the floor—an easy task for her, since she was so small. While she did her chores, Katanya sang. She had a beautiful voice that sounded as if a full-grown girl were singing. Katanya's voice filled the city with gladness, bringing joy to everyone who heard it.

One day a prince was riding down the street, when he heard a lovely song drifting from an open window. The voice was so beautiful that he fell instantly in love. When he returned to the palace, he told his father, the king: "Father, I have found a lovely bride, and I wish to be married."

"Very well, my son," said the king in surprise, "but who is the bride?"

"I wish to marry the girl whose beautiful singing I heard today," said the prince.

The king sent a servant at once to the house of the old woman and invited her to come with her daughter to the palace. The servant told the woman: "I have brought a tailor with me who will sew dresses for you both."

But when the old woman told Katanya this, the girl shook her head. "No, no, no! I love my dress of many colors, and that's what I will wear." So the tailor fitted the old woman, but when he asked to see the girl, he was told that she already had a pretty dress.

A few days later, the old woman put on her new dress and went to the palace, with Katanya hiding inside the pocket. The king welcomed her, but the prince was very sad. "Your daughter was invited to join us too," he said. "Why has she not come?"

All at once a tiny voice came from the pocket: "Here I am!" Then Katanya's head peeked out.

"Is it you I heard singing?" asked the prince, much amazed.

"Perhaps," she answered.

"In that case," said the prince, "could you sing for us now? If you are the girl I heard, then it is you I want to marry, even though you are small."

Katanya smiled, for what the prince said was very nice indeed. And she sang a song more beautiful than any he had ever heard.

So it was that Katanya married the prince and became Princess Katanya. At her wedding she wore her favorite dress of many colors. And the old woman came to live at the palace along with her. And all of them—the prince, Katanya, and her mother—lived happily ever after.

TURKEY: ORAL TRADITION

THE MAGIC SANDALS
OF ABU KASSIM

THERE ONCE was a man named Abu Kassim who lived far away in the land of Turkey. He made his living by selling rags, and although he worked hard, luck was against him and he was very poor. Every morning Abu Kassim would walk along the street, calling, "Rags for sale! Rags for sale! Come and buy my rags!" But no one wanted them, and soon Abu Kassim grew so poor that he had only one torn shirt, one ragged pair of pants, and no shoes at all to put on his feet.

One day, after Abu Kassim had been walking all morning, trying to sell his rags, he sat down at the side of a road to rest. He opened the small sack his wife had given him and took out the piece of crusty bread that was his lunch.

As he did, he noticed an old man with a long white beard coming toward him, looking tired indeed. "Good day, Grandfather," said Abu Kassim.

"Good day," answered the old man.

"Please," said Abu Kassim, "you look so tired. Won't you sit down beside me and rest?" Then Abu Kassim held out his piece of bread. "Here, take this," he said. "You must be hungry. I wish I had more to offer you, but this is all I have."

The old man thankfully accepted the bread of Abu Kassim and ate it slowly; he didn't waste a single crumb. When he had finished, he turned to Abu Kassim and said, "Abu Kassim, you have a kind heart, and I have the power to grant you a special wish. Ask for anything you want, and it shall be yours."

Abu Kassim was startled. "Oh, if only I had a pair of shoes," he sighed. At once, as if by magic, the man drew out of Abu Kassim's sack of rags a pair of shiny new sandals.

"Thank you, thank you," cried Abu Kassim in disbelief. Without delay he put on his new shoes. How comfortable they were! How quickly Abu Kassim could walk in them! He knew at once that they were the most wonderful sandals he had ever had or could ever hope to have—and he turned to thank the old man for such a fine gift. But when he looked up, the old man was gone.

From the very moment that Abu Kassim put on those sandals, his luck began to change. Soon he was walking

more quickly than ever, still calling loudly, "Rags for sale! Rags for sale! Come and buy my rags!" But now more and more people bought the rags, and Abu Kassim was taking gold coins home every day. Some he was able to save, and before long he opened a fine shop. There he sold fine hats and shirts and pants, and he charged prices so low that even the poorest people could afford them.

People came to his shop from all corners of the city. Months passed. Years passed. Abu Kassim grew rich. He built a large house, wore the finest clothes, and ate the most delicious foods. And he always remembered to share with those who were poor.

Now, all this time, Abu Kassim wore his beautiful sandals. But as time went on, the sandals began to wear out. There was a hole here, a tear there, a creak here, a squeak there, a rip here, a crack there.

One day when Abu Kassim was walking near his shop, he met a neighbor. "Abu Kassim," said the neighbor, "what a fine shirt you have! Such new pants! Such a wonderful embroidered cap! But, for shame, look at your ragged shoes! What a disgrace!"

Abu Kassim looked at his sandals, and he was ashamed. "My neighbor is right," he said to himself. "I must get rid of these shabby sandals. But how?" The next day Abu Kassim went to a shoe shop and bought a shiny new pair of sandals. Then he walked home past a river—and threw his old pair into the water. He watched as the sandals sank to the bottom, happy to be rid of them.

But the very next morning, who should appear at his door but two fishermen. "Abu Kassim! Abu Kassim!" they cried. "See what we have found in our nets!" They held out Abu Kassim's old sandals, water dripping from their holes.

Oh no, thought Abu Kassim, but he thanked the fishermen politely and sent them on their way. I must get rid of these shoes somehow, he thought.

So Abu Kassim went to the bath house, his sandals tucked tightly under his arm. "I will leave the sandals here," he said to himself. "Perhaps someone will pick them up and take them home." Then he returned to his house, pleased to be rid of the sandals.

But the very next morning who should appear at his door but a small boy. "Abu Kassim! Abu Kassim!" he cried. "You left your sandals at the bath house, and I have brought them back." The boy held up Abu Kassim's old shoes.

"Oh no," said Abu Kassim to himself, but he thanked the boy politely and sent him on his way.

By this time Abu Kassim was desperate. "How can I get rid of these sandals?" he wondered. Finally he got an idea. He waited until the sun set and the sky grew dark.

Then he took a shovel, went to a big field, and dug a hole. "I will bury those sandals so deep that no one will find them," he said. And so he did. And as Abu Kassim walked home, he smiled, for he had gotten rid of the sandals at last.

But the very next morning who should appear at his door but two policemen, looking very stern. "Abu Kassim," they said, "last night someone saw you burying a treasure in a field. That land belongs to the Sultan, so the treasure belongs to him as well. You must dig it up at once!"

Abu Kassim laughed to himself and led the policemen to where the "treasure" was buried. And when the policemen saw Abu Kassim's shabby old sandals, full of dirt, they laughed too.

"It seems," said Abu Kassim, "that these sandals and I cannot be parted from each other." He shook the dirt from his sandals and put them on.

Oh, they were as comfortable as ever! With them on, Abu Kassim could walk even more quickly than before. "My dear sandals," he said, "I do not know what I did to deserve you, but you are certainly the best present I have ever been given!"

Then Abu Kassim knew that the old man who had given him the magic sandals was Elijah the Prophet, who is sent by God to help the Jews when they are in need.

Abu Kassim wore those sandals for as long as he lived, for no matter how many holes and rips, tears and cracks they had, and how many creaks and squeaks they made, those sandals never wore out. And Abu Kassim's good luck and good fortune stayed with him always.

TURKEY: ORAL TRADITION

THE WATER WITCH

ONCE UPON A TIME there were two children who went down to the sea every morning to throw bread crumbs on the water. The children were so poor that they barely had enough food for themselves. But they remembered the words in the Bible: *Cast your bread on the waters, for a time will come when you will find it again.*

The girl's name was Hava, which means Eve, and the boy's name was Shlomo, which means Solomon, and they were the children of a poor boatmaker and his wife.

Every morning Shlomo and Hava would run down to the shore and watch for the same fish who came each day to eat their bread crumbs. As they watched, day after day, that fish grew bigger and bigger—until it was the biggest fish they had ever seen.

Now not far from shore lived a water witch, who saw the good deed that the children did every day. And every day her heart grew blacker because she couldn't bear to see good deeds being done.

One day, after the big fish left, the witch called, "Children, children, come closer so you can hear me." The children looked around but could see no one.

The witch called again, "Here, here in the sea!" So Shlomo and Hava looked across the waves and saw the witch rising up out of the water—smoking a pipe! They could hardly believe their eyes. How could a pipe stay lit when it was wet? They walked to the very edge of the water to see how such a thing could happen.

That is exactly what the witch had been waiting for. Quickly she threw a magic net around them and dragged them, kicking and screaming, deep beneath the sea. But the children didn't drown. The magic net was like a big bubble filled with air, so they could still breathe inside it.

The witch dragged the net all the way down to the ocean floor, to a little cage she had built there. Then she pushed the net inside, with the children still trapped in it. Finally she locked the cage door. "You are my prisoners," she cackled. And she disappeared, leaving the children all alone.

Shlomo and Hava were frightened. Who could find them there—trapped in a cage at the bottom of the sea?

They were hungry too. Shlomo reached into his pocket and found two carobs that he had picked on his way to the shore that morning. One he gave to Hava and one he kept for himself. The two nibbled on the carobs slowly, so as not to use up their small supply of food.

When the children did not return home that day, their mother and father ran down to the shore crying, "Shlomo! Hava! Where are you?" But the children were nowhere to be seen.

The next morning the big fish came back to the shore for his daily food, but the children who fed him bread crumbs were not there. Where can they be? he wondered. The fish swam from one place to another, asking all the other fish, "Have you seen the children who give me bread every day?" From the other fish he soon learned what the wicked witch had done.

Then the big fish swam quickly to the palace beneath the sea where the great whale Leviathan, King of the Sea, ruled the ocean.

"My lord of the sea, a terrible thing has happened," he told the king. "Two kind children have been kidnapped by the water witch and imprisoned at the bottom of the sea. Please help me set them free."

"Yes, it's time to stop the evil water witch!" said Leviathan. "Here is a seashell, and inside it is a magic stone. Take it to the children and tell them that whatever the stone touches that is alive will die. But whatever the stone touches that is dead will be brought to life."

The big fish took the seashell in his mouth, and off he swam.

The children were sobbing in each other's arms when they saw their friend, the big fish, swimming their way. The fish circled the cage several times, then spit the seashell out of his mouth and into their little prison. Shlomo picked up the seashell and was just about to turn it over when, to the children's amazement, the fish spoke.

"Fear not," said their friend, "for inside that seashell is a magic stone, sent to you by Leviathan, King of the Sea. Whatever that stone touches that is alive will die, but whatever the stone touches that is dead will be brought to life. Surely you can use it to save yourselves." The children were filled with joy, for now they had reason to hope again.

The fish swam away, but Shlomo and Hava remained there all day long. Another day passed, and another, and still the witch did not come back. The children were growing hungry and weak, for the carobs were all gone. But as they waited, they thought of a plan.

On the evening of the third day, the water witch returned, certain that the children had starved to death. When Shlomo and Hava saw the witch coming, they both lay down and closed their eyes, pretending to be dead.

The witch laughed to herself and took out the key. "So, my little dears, now that you are dead, I can use the net to

capture other children." But the moment the witch opened the gate, Shlomo and Hava quickly sat up.

My, how the witch was surprised! "I didn't leave you even a crumb of food. How can it be that you are still alive?" she demanded.

"Oh," answered Shlomo, "we have a magic stone inside this shell. Whenever we are hungry, we only have to rub the stone, and it gives us all we need to eat."

"Give it to me!" shrieked the witch.

"It's mine!" Shlomo cried.

The witch snatched the shell from Shlomo's hands. But the moment she touched the magic stone, she fell down dead. Then the big fish, who had been hiding nearby, swam to the open door of the cage. "Drag the witch inside," the fish called out. The children didn't know why the fish wanted them to do this, but he was their friend, so they obeyed.

Next the fish said, "Pick up the key and come out. Then lock the door." And again the children did what the fish requested.

"Now reach between the bars of the cage," the fish told them, "and use the seashell to push the magic stone against the arm of the witch—but be sure not to touch the stone yourself!"

Shlomo did as he was told and quickly pulled his arm back. At once the witch sat up, and when she found herself locked in the cage, oh, she was furious.

"Give me the key!" she shouted. Instead, Shlomo tossed the key to the fish—who swallowed it!

The big fish took the net into his mouth and pulled it to the shore of the sea. There the children climbed out, waved good-bye to the fish, and ran home as fast as they could. How happy their mother and father were to see them!

After that, Shlomo and Hava returned to the shore every day to feed bread crumbs to their friend the fish. And never again were they bothered by the evil water witch.

THE ORIENT: c. NINTH–ELEVENTH CENTURIES

THE ENORMOUS FROG

ONCE THERE was an enormous frog as big as sixty cities. Imagine how big that frog was!

Then came a snake with a tail so long it could circle the world, and it swallowed the frog that was as big as sixty cities. Imagine how big that snake was!

Then came a raven that covered the sky like a dark cloud, and it swallowed the snake with the tail so long it could circle the world, which swallowed the frog as big as sixty cities. Imagine how big that raven was!

And up flew the raven and sat on the branch of a tree whose highest branches touched the sky. Imagine how big that tree was!

Then came a giant who cut down the tree whose top branches touched the sky, where sat the raven that covered the sky like a dark cloud, which swallowed the snake whose tail circled the world, which swallowed the frog that was as big as sixty cities. Imagine how big that giant was! And the tree came tumbling down.

Then came a voice from far above, calling out the giant's name. Imagine that!

BABYLON: c. FIFTH CENTURY

A TALE OF TWO CHICKENS

THERE ONCE lived a rabbi named Hanina ben Dosa. This rabbi was known by all to be a very honest man.

One day it happened that a merchant on his way to market lost two chickens near Rabbi Hanina's house. The rabbi's wife found the chickens and took care of them. But though they were very poor, Rabbi Hanina told his wife, "These chickens do not belong to us, and we may not eat their eggs."

Now these chickens laid a great many eggs, and this caused Rabbi Hanina to be greatly troubled. "What should I do? It is not right for me to eat these eggs, for the chickens are not mine—but, on the other hand, I don't want the eggs to go to waste."

So Rabbi Hanina sold the eggs. With the money he got

[65]

from them, he bought two goats. Before long the goats gave birth, and there were four goats instead of two. These goats gave delicious milk, but Rabbi Hanina told his wife, "These goats really do not belong to us, and we may not drink their milk."

The goats gave more and more milk, and this caused Rabbi Hanina to be greatly troubled. "What should I do? It is not right for me to drink this milk, for the goats are not mine—but, on the other hand, I don't want the milk to go to waste."

So Rabbi Hanina sold the goats' milk. With the money he got from it, he bought two cows. Before long the cows gave birth, and then there were four cows instead of two. And Rabbi Hanina took care of the four cows, but he and his wife did not drink their milk. "After all, these cows do not belong to us," he said.

Instead, Rabbi Hanina's wife made cheese from the milk, but still Rabbi Hanina was greatly troubled. "What should I do? It is not right for me to eat this cheese, for the cows are not mine—but, on the other hand, I don't want the cheese to go to waste."

So Rabbi Hanina sold the cheese. The money he got from it he gave to the poor.

One day the same merchant who had lost the chickens stopped at Rabbi Hanina's house. "By chance, dear rabbi,

did you find two chickens I lost a long time ago?" he asked.

Rabbi Hanina brought out the two plump chickens, which were strutting about happily, looking very healthy indeed. He also brought out the four goats and the four cows, and gave them to the man.

The merchant was quite surprised. "But rabbi, I lost only two chickens. Why are you giving me goats and cows?"

"Ah," said Rabbi Hanina ben Dosa, "you see, since the chickens belong to you, everything that came about because of them belongs to you as well."

The man was amazed. "Rabbi Hanina," he said, "I can see that you are a very honest man. If not for you, I would have nothing at all. Therefore, please accept two goats as a reward for your help."

"Oh no," said Rabbi Hanina. "I was only doing what was right by taking care of your chickens. I cannot accept a reward."

But the merchant insisted. So Rabbi Hanina took the goats and thanked the man for his gift. Then, with the chickens clucking in his arms, the goats bleating, and the cows mooing, the merchant walked happily back home.

As for the two goats that he gave to Rabbi Hanina,

why, they soon had baby goats, and Rabbi Hanina found that he had much sweet milk to sell. Before long he had enough money to share with all who came to him for help. And so it was that God rewarded Rabbi Hanina for being honest.

BABYLON: c. FIFTH CENTURY

A PALACE OF BIRD BEAKS

THERE ONCE was a king named Solomon, who was known throughout the world for his wisdom. Why, he could command the winds and birds to come whenever he called them. He even knew the language of every bird and animal on earth.

Now it so happened that King Solomon's wife was soon to have a birthday. The king asked her what gift she would like.

"Oh, I would like something that no other queen on earth has ever had," she said. "Build me a palace of bird beaks!"

And out of love for his wife, Solomon answered, "You shall have it, my dear. A palace of bird beaks shall be yours."

Then King Solomon called forth all the birds in the world and ordered them to come to his palace, prepared to give up their beaks. Before even a day had gone by, thousands of birds filled the sky, beating their wings and swooping down to the palace. All came: the strong eagle, the tiny hummingbird, the bluebird, the mockingbird, and every bird that lived on earth. The birds were not very happy at having to give up their beaks. But what could they do? They were among the smallest creatures in the kingdom. Soon every bird had flocked to the palace except one—the hoopoe—a little bird with colorful feathers and a fine, pointed beak. As time passed and it did not arrive, the king became angry.

"Fetch the hoopoe and bring it here!" he shouted to his servants. "Let it be punished for failing to obey the king!"

At last the hoopoe was brought before the king.

"Where have you been?" King Solomon demanded. "Why have you kept me waiting?"

"Please, your Majesty, do not be angry with me," said the hoopoe. "I have been flying to the ends of the earth. I have seen gardens, forests, oceans, deserts—and from all that I have seen, I have gained much wisdom, so that I may serve you well. Punish me if you must, but first give me a chance to prove that I have not just been flying lazily about. Let me ask you three riddles. If you can answer correctly, then do what you will with me. But if there is even one of them that you cannot answer, then spare my life."

The other birds gasped. How shocked they were that a

bird dared bargain with the king! But King Solomon admired this bold little creature, and he accepted the challenge. "Very well," he said, "ask your riddles. After all, how can your wisdom be compared to the wisdom of a king?"

So the hoopoe spoke. "This is the first riddle. Tell me, your Majesty, who is it who was never born and has never died?"

The king did not even pause to think.

"The Lord of the world, blessed be He," he said at once. And as he spoke, King Solomon thought, The Lord of the world who created all creatures to be free.

The hoopoe continued. "Here is the second riddle. Tell me, your Majesty, what water never rises from the ground and never falls from the sky?"

King Solomon smiled, for he knew the answer. "The answer is a tear," he said, "a tear that falls from an eye that cries with sadness." And as he finished answering, King Solomon looked around and saw all those birds stretched out before him, waiting sadly and helplessly for their beaks to be cut off. The king too was saddened, and a tear came to his eye.

Now a strange thing happened. Although King Solomon was certain that his wisdom was perfect, for just a moment it occurred to him that perhaps he had done a foolish thing in agreeing to build a palace of bird beaks.

Then the hoopoe spoke again, and this time it trembled, for it had only one riddle left—only one more chance to save itself.

"Your Majesty, what is it that is delicate enough to put food in a baby's mouth, yet strong enough to bore holes in the hardest wood?"

It did not take King Solomon long to reply. "Why, a bird's beak, of course!" he answered. And looking around at that great gathering of birds, he realized how special those creatures were, and how very precious their beaks were to them.

Meanwhile the hoopoe bowed its head. "Punish me as you will, your Majesty, for you have answered my three riddles." And it waited in silence to hear the harsh punishment of the king.

But the king was smiling. "Dear hoopoe," he announced in a loud voice, so that all the birds could hear, "I am known throughout the world for my wisdom, yet you are the one who is truly wise, You have shown me that a king should never be too proud to admit he has made a mistake. I have decided not to build a palace of bird beaks after all!"

At this, all the birds wanted to flap their wings in joy, but they did not dare to interrupt the king.

"For your wisdom you shall be rewarded, not punished," said King Solomon. He called forth the royal

[74]

jeweler and bade him make the bird a small crown, much like the crown that he himself, the king, wore upon his head. And when the crown was finished, King Solomon placed it upon the head of the hoopoe.

So it is that to this day the hoopoe wears a crown on its forehead, to remind all the birds who see it of the reward of King Solomon and the wisdom of the bird who saved their beaks.

YEMEN: ORAL TRADITION

THE DIAMOND TREE

ONCE UPON A TIME there was a man named Nissim who was very poor. He was so poor that the tiny hut he and his family lived in didn't even have any water. To get water for himself and for his family, he had to walk many miles to a river. There he would fill a barrel with water, lift it onto his back, and carry the heavy barrel all the way home. And by the time he got there, the sky would be dark, and the tired man would go to sleep.

Now one day Nissim carried home a barrel of water as usual, but the next morning, when he went out to get the water, the barrel was empty. "What could have happened to the water?" he said to himself. He went back to the river and filled his barrel once more. But in the morning, when he looked into the barrel, again not a drop of water was left.

The same thing happened three days in a row, and at

last Nissim became angry. "Enough of this! Tonight I will hide in my barrel and see who is stealing my water."

So it was that Nissim was inside the barrel at midnight when two eagles swooped down from the sky and picked it up in their huge claws. They flew a long distance, while Nissim shivered in fear. "What if they should drop me from this great height?" he thought.

Finally he felt the barrel come to rest on the ground. "Thank God that I am safe," he said aloud.

When the dizzy man peeked out, the first thing he saw was the sea, far below, for the barrel had landed on a high cliff. Then he looked up and saw that the eagles had flown to a nest way up in the branches of a tree—and lo and behold, the tree was full of diamonds!

Now, when the eagles saw a man peeking out of the barrel, they were quite surprised and flew down to him.

"Please, please don't hurt me," begged Nissim.

"We won't," said the first eagle. "You see, we're not really eagles at all. We're children. The witch who owns the diamond tree came to our land and kidnapped us. Then she cast a spell upon us all."

"There are other children here?" asked Nissim in amazement.

"Many," replied the eagle. "First the witch turns us into eagles and sends us far away to bring water for her tree. Then, when we grow too weak to carry the water,

she turns us into diamonds."

"We only want to be children again and go back to our mothers and fathers," cried the second eagle. "Won't you help us?"

"Of course I will," said Nissim, "but where can I find the witch?"

"Right here!" shrieked a terrible voice. Nissim looked up, and there, standing right in front of him, was a frightful, ugly witch. "Who are you, my dear man, a new eagle to bring water to my diamond tree?" she cackled.

Nissim knew that he must do something quickly or he too would be turned into an eagle. "I don't believe you," he said boldly. "I don't think you have the power to turn *anyone* into an eagle."

"You're a fool," snapped the witch. "It's the easiest thing in the world."

"Well, I won't believe it," Nissim said, "unless I see it with my own eyes. I'm sure you can't turn these eagles back into children."

"Ha!" said the witch. "Just wait and see!" And she began to chant:

"Eagles in the sky, diamonds on the tree,
       whether eagles or children is up to me!
Turn back to a child for as long as I say,
       whether for an hour or for a day!"

[81]

All at once the two eagles became a boy and a girl. How happy they were to be children again!

"Now do you believe me?" asked the witch, pointing her crooked finger at Nissim.

"Not really," he answered. "If you were a great witch, you could also turn the diamonds back into children."

The witch scowled and walked over to the tree. "Just watch!" she cried. She plucked one of the diamonds and chanted another spell:

"Eagles in the sky, diamonds on the tree,
      whether diamonds or children is up to me!
Turn back to a child for as long as I say,
      whether for an hour or for a day!"

And lo and behold, a third child stood there before him, astonished to be a girl again.

"Now are you convinced?" sneered the witch, quite proud of herself.

"Not yet," said Nissim. "Why, if your powers were really great, you could turn *yourself* into a diamond as well. Then I would know that you were truly the most powerful witch in all the world."

When the witch heard that, her eyes grew narrow. "I'll show you!" she shrieked. And she began to chant again:

[82]

"Eagles in the sky, diamonds on the tree,
  no trick in the world is too difficult for me!
I'll turn into a diamond to show you who I am,
  and then I'll finish you off, you foolish man!"

Suddenly, as Nissim watched, a new diamond appeared on the tree, far bigger than any of the others. It was not white like the other diamonds, but blood red.

Without waiting an instant, Nissim plucked the big red diamond from the tree and threw it as hard and as far as he could, into the sea. When the diamond struck the water, it burst into flames and disappeared. At the same instant, all the diamonds on the tree turned into children. How they cheered and hugged each other when they learned that the evil witch was dead! They thanked Nissim again and again for saving them. "Thank God that you are safe," he answered.

Then one young girl looked at him sadly. "But how will we get home?" she asked.

Nissim thought for a moment. "We will have to get home by ourselves," he said. "Let us cut down the diamond tree and use its wood to build a boat."

"Yes, yes, we will all help!" cried the children at once, and they found an axe for him to use. When Nissim had chopped down the tree, he noticed that the trunk was hollow. Inside was a treasure chest filled with diamonds that the witch had hidden there—*real* diamonds this time. Nissim gave a big diamond to each of the children and kept one for himself—there were just the right number of diamonds to go around. Then he and the children built a fine boat from the trunk of the tree.

When the boat was ready, they all pushed and pulled it down to the sea. Back they sailed to the shore of their land, singing happily all the way. And Nissim saw to it that each and every child reached home safely.

Then Nissim went back to his home too, and kissed his wife and children. "Thank God that you are safe!" they said. He sold his diamond, and with some of the money he built a new house with a fine, deep well beside it—never again did Nissim have to carry water from the river. With some of the money he helped build a new synagogue in his city. The rest of the money he shared with those who were poor, as he had once been.

And what of the children? Why, they came often to visit Nissim and his family, and they were all the best of friends for as long as they lived.

MOROCCO: ORAL TRADITION

MOVING A MOUNTAIN

NOW WHEN GOD created the world, He planned to put a few foolish people in every place. But the angel who was carrying out God's plan was surprised by a crack of thunder, and dropped a whole sack full of foolish souls in one place—a little city in Poland called Chelm.

Because of this accident, everything in Chelm was turned upside down, and the townsfolk thought that the most foolish people were really the wisest of them all. Whenever the people had problems and didn't know how to solve them, they ran to these "wise" men for help. The wise men of Chelm—who were named Beryl, Shmerel, Moishe, and Oysher—would think very hard and wrinkle their foreheads, and then they would give their wise advice.

One summer it was very hot in Chelm. There was not even the slightest bit of a breeze. The men couldn't work, the women couldn't bake, and the babies cried all night long. The townsfolk didn't know what to do, so they went to the wise men for guidance.

"What shall we do?" they cried. "It is so hot that we cannot work, we cannot bake, we cannot sleep." The wise men listened to the problem. They wrinkled their foreheads. And then Beryl spoke.

"The answer to your problem is this: Near our city of Chelm are high mountains. On top of the mountains there is still snow left from winter. All you townsfolk of Chelm must go to the mountains and fill your pockets with as much snow as you can carry! Then, when you return to Chelm, you can use the snow to keep cool."

The townsfolk listened. "How wonderful!" they cried. "What wise advice!"

And off they went to the mountains: Men, women, and babies, led by the rabbi himself. The townsfolk filled their pockets with clean white snow and walked back to Chelm. But when they got there, the snow was gone—it had all melted!

"Oh dear," they cried. "What shall we do now?" Back they went to the wise men of Chelm.

"We are still hot," they cried. "We cannot work, we

cannot bake, we cannot sleep. Oh, please, please, tell us what to do."

The wise men listened again. This time they wrinkled their foreheads more deeply than before. And then Shmerel spoke.

"The problem," he said, "is that the sun is shining so brightly, it is making you hot. You must fool the sun and make it think that it is winter."

"How can we do that?" asked the townsfolk.

"It's simple!" answered Moishe. "You must all go home, put on your heaviest clothes—fur coats and sweaters, hats and boots, gloves and mittens—and stand outside. Then, when the sun looks down and sees you dressed so warmly, it will think that it's winter and go away."

"How clever!" cried everyone, jumping up and down with joy. The townsfolk ran home, put on their heaviest clothes—fur coats, sweaters, hats, boots, gloves, mittens—and stood outside in front of the synagogue. Even the babies were bundled up. And there they waited, all together, standing in the sun.

Soon they began to sweat. They got hotter and hotter. The babies cried louder. The sun was not fooled. Finally the townsfolk ran to the wise men of Chelm.

"Oh, things are even worse than before," they cried.

"We are still hot. We cannot work. We cannot bake. We cannot sleep. Please, please, tell us what to do."

The wise men listened, and thought even harder than ever. Their foreheads wrinkled even more deeply. At last Oysher spoke. "I have an idea," he said.

"Oh, what is it? Tell us, tell us, please," begged the townsfolk.

"It seems," said Oysher the Wise, "that if there is no breeze in Chelm, it must be because the mountain just outside Chelm is blocking the breeze and keeping it from coming here. You must choose the two strongest men in Chelm and send them to move the mountain."

"Oh, yes, yes," the people cried. "This time the plan will surely work." And they left in great excitement, certain that their terrible problem would soon be solved.

Now, everyone knew that the strongest men in Chelm were Mendel the butcher and Lemel the porter. The two were called forth, and the very next morning they set out to move the mountain.

They began to push. They pushed and pushed—and pushed some more. For one hour, two, three, they toiled.

The sun shone down on them. Sweat poured down their faces. They got hotter and hotter. But they didn't stop for even one moment, for, after all, they had an important job to do.

At noon the rabbi's wife brought them fresh cold borscht and sour cream. The men stopped pushing long enough to refresh themselves with this wonderful soup, and afterward they took off their shirts and threw them on the ground. Then they returned to work.

Mendel pushed, and Lemel pushed. They pushed and pushed with all their might, and while they were busy pushing, along came a thief. Seeing the nice shirts lying on the ground, he picked them up and ran away.

Still the men pushed. Suddenly Mendel looked down at the ground. The shirts were gone. "Lemel, Lemel," he cried, "our shirts are missing!"

Lemel stopped pushing and looked at the ground. Mendel was right. "Where can they be?" he cried. "How can we get them back?"

The two men looked at the ground, then at each other. They had no way to solve the problem. So what did they do? They ran off to see the wise men of Chelm.

The wise men listened to the problem, but this time they did not have to wrinkle their foreheads for very long. The answer was a simple one.

"Lemel and Mendel," they said, "you have done a great deed for the people of Chelm. Soon the breeze will begin to blow, and no longer will the townsfolk be hot—

[91]

for, if you can no longer see your shirts, you have pushed the mountain very far indeed!"

And when the people heard the good news that the mountain had been moved, they all cheered and celebrated and gave thanks that their town had been blessed with such wise men.

POLAND: ORAL TRADITION

THE BEAR AND
THE CHILDREN

THERE ONCE was a rabbi and his wife who had seven children, and they loved each and every one of them very much. One day the rabbi went to the synagogue and his wife went to gather blueberries. But before they left, they said to their children: "Now remember, never, never let anyone into the house when we're not here." And this the children promised.

But not long after the father and mother left, a great big bear came to the house and knocked on the door. "Open up, my dear children," said the bear sweetly. "Your father is here."

"Oh, no. You are not our father," the children called back. "Our father has gone to the synagogue." So the bear went back into the woods.

A short time later he knocked on the door again. "Open the door, my dear children. Your mother is here," he said sweetly.

"Oh no. You are not our mother. Our mother has gone to pick blueberries." So the bear went back into the woods again.

Soon he knocked on the door a third time. "Open up, children—or I'll break your door down!"

Now all the children were terrified, and they ran to hide as fast as they could. The first hid behind the stove; the second jumped in the washtub; the third hid in the closet; the fourth crawled under the bed; the fifth hid under a coat; the sixth squeezed behind a mirror; and the seventh and youngest child jumped in his bed and pulled the covers over his head. How frightened they were when the bear broke the door down!

Then the bear ran from one hiding place to another, snatching up each child as he went and swallowing each one in a single gulp. He snatched the first one, hidden behind the stove, and then the second, hidden in the washtub, the third, hidden in the closet, and the fourth, under the bed, the fifth, wrapped in the coat, and finally the sixth, squeezed behind the mirror. But he did not think to look in the bed of the youngest child, where the seventh was hiding beneath the covers.

When the rabbi and his wife came back, they found the door broken down and all their children gone. They ran through the house, calling each child by name. "Where are you? Where are you?" But they got no answer—until they called the youngest one. Out he climbed from under the covers, and he told them how the bear had swallowed all his brothers and sisters.

The children's mother did not waste even one moment. She took a knife, a jar of honey, some loaves of bread, and a needle and thread. Then she ran off into the woods, calling the bear as she went:

"Bear, bear,
  come here.
  I have blueberries for you."

But the bear did not come. So she called:

"Bear, bear,
  come here.
  I have noodles with milk."

But the bear did not come. So she called:

"Bear, bear,
  come here.
  I have honey for you."

When the bear heard this, he came at once, for he loved honey more than anything else in the world. After he had eaten all the honey, he was full, so he lay down and fell asleep. And as soon as he was asleep, the mother took the knife and cut the bear open. Out jumped the children:

[95]

one, two, three, four, five, six—until they all stood there in front of her, as good as new.

The mother then tossed the six loaves of bread into the bear's belly and sewed him up again. "Come, children," she said, "run home with me as fast as you can."

This the children gladly did. They ran all the way home and got there safe and sound long before the bear woke up. Their father hugged them and promised he would put up a door so strong that no bear could ever break it down. Then their mother washed every one of them from top to bottom, until they were as clean as a whistle. And when the bear awoke, his belly was full, and he was perfectly happy—but not as happy as the six children who had just escaped from that very same place!

EASTERN EUROPE: ORAL TRADITION

THE GOBLIN

ONCE there was a goblin who lived in the cellar of a house. But that goblin didn't stay in the cellar. No! It sneaked upstairs so it could hide the keys, poke holes in the milk pitcher, and crow like a rooster.

At breakfast it made the fried eggs jump off the table and slide under the dog. At lunch it turned plates of food upside down, and at dinner it made wine bubble over the tops of glasses.

And worst of all, on the Sabbath it threw little stones inside the menorahs, so the wife couldn't put the candles in place.

Now the people who lived in that house were very worried. "We must get rid of that evil imp," they said. They hung magic charms on the windows and wrote holy names on the walls. But nothing helped.

The water barrel tipped over by itself and all the water

spilled out. Knocking was heard on the windows, and wild laughter came from the roof. And sometimes smoke came from the fireplace when no fire had been lit. The pranks went on without end.

Then one day a Hasid, who was passing through the city, was tricked into spending the night in that very house. Being a holy man, he awoke at midnight and lit a candle so he could say the midnight prayers.

No sooner was the candle lit than the goblin blew it out.

The Hasid tried to light the candle again, and again the goblin blew it out.

The Hasid was annoyed, but he got up to light the candle once more. And once more the goblin blew it out. This time the goblin made a horrible growling sound that would have terrified anyone else. But not the Hasid.

For the faith of the Hasid was strong. Instead of running away, he cried, "Get away from here, evil one— or I will finish you!"

But the goblin wasn't frightened, not one bit. It stood right beside the Hasid and stuck out its tongue.

Though the Hasid could not see or hear the goblin, he could sense its evil presence. He picked up his prayer book and swung it in the darkness. And he hit that goblin right on the head.

The instant the holy letters touched the evil creature,

its power vanished, and it was filled with fear. And the goblin hurried down the stairs to the cellar, jumped through a hole in the wall, and never, ever came back again.

EASTERN EUROPE: NINETEENTH CENTURY

THE PRINCE WHO THOUGHT
HE WAS A ROOSTER

THERE ONCE was a prince who thought he was a rooster. While other princes spent their days slaying dragons, courting princesses, or learning how to rule a kingdom, this prince cast off his royal robes and spent his days crouching beneath a table, refusing to eat any food except kernels of corn.

His father, the king, was very upset at this behavior. "Send for the best doctors in all the land," he proclaimed. "A great reward will be given to anyone who can cure my son."

Doctors came from all corners of the kingdom. Each tried to cure the prince, but not one of them succeeded. The prince still thought he was a rooster. He ate corn, preened his feathers, and strutted about, crying, "Cock-a-doodle-do! Cock-a-doodle-do!"

[101]

When the king had almost given up hope, a wise man, passing through the kingdom, appeared before him. "Let me stay alone with the prince for one week, and I will cure him," he said to the king.

"Everyone else has failed," the king moaned, "but you are welcome to try."

Thus the wise man entered the prince's chamber. There he took off his clothes, crawled under the table, and began to eat kernels of corn, just like the prince.

The prince looked at the man with suspicion. "Who are you?" he asked.

"I am a rooster," said the wise man, and he continued to munch the corn. After a short while he asked, "Who are you?"

"I, too, am a rooster," said the prince.

And after that the prince treated the wise man as an equal. The two strutted about, preening their feathers and crying, "Cock-a-doodle-do! Cock-a-doodle-do!"

When they had made their home under the table for a while and had become good friends, the wise man suddenly crawled out into the prince's chamber and dressed himself.

The prince was shocked.

"A rooster doesn't wear clothes!" he said.

The wise man remained calm. "I am a rooster and I am wearing clothes!"

The prince considered this for a day or two. Then he decided to imitate his friend, and he, too, put on clothes.

A few days later, the wise man took some of the food that was being delivered to them every day, food that they had refused to eat. He carried it beneath the table and ate it.

The prince was astonished. "Roosters don't eat that kind of food!"

But the wise man calmly said, "A rooster can eat any food he wants and still be a good rooster." And he continued to eat the tasty food.

The prince watched this for a while. Then he decided to imitate his friend, and he, too, ate the food.

The next day the wise man stopped crouching beneath the table. He stood up proudly on his two feet and started to walk like a man.

"What are you doing?" asked the prince. "A rooster can't get up and walk around like that!"

But the wise man said firmly, "I am a rooster, and if I want to walk like this, I will!" And he continued to walk upright.

The prince peered at him from beneath the table. Then he decided to imitate his friend and he, too, stood up and walked on his two feet.

So, in this way, the prince began to eat, dress, and walk like a man. The week's time was up, and no longer did he act like a rooster. The king was overjoyed, of course, and welcomed his son back with open arms.

As for the wise man, why, he collected his reward and went happily on his way.

EASTERN EUROPE: NINETEENTH CENTURY

THE ANGEL'S WINGS

LONG AGO, before the days of Noah and the ark, there lived a young girl whose name was Istahar. She was beautiful and kind and wise, and she always tried to do what was right.

Istahar loved to watch the moon and the stars at night. When the sun set, she could hardly wait for the sky to grow dark and the stars to come out. Then she would sit down on the ground next to a tree and stare up into the heavens.

What Istahar loved most of all was to see a falling star. When she did, she would try to follow that star until it disappeared from sight. She wondered where falling stars went, and said to herself, "Oh, I wish more than anything that I could have one for my own."

One night Istahar's wish came true. She was sitting under her favorite tree when she saw a star fall. She sat up very straight and watched it closely as it raced through the sky. But this time the star did not disappear. Instead, the whole earth suddenly lit up, and there was a sound like a great wind. All at once the night grew dark again—except something was glowing in the branches of the very tree Istahar was leaning against, as if the moon had slipped inside the branches.

When Istahar saw that bright, glowing light, she was certain that a star had fallen into the tree. And when she saw how beautifully it shone, she knew she had to have it for her very own. Why, it cast a light that completely surrounded her, and in that light she felt as if she herself were glowing, as if she herself were a star.

Feeling very sure of herself, Istahar climbed up into the tree. She reached out and oh, so carefully—for she was afraid that it might be burning hot—touched the glowing object with her finger. Much to her surprise, though, it felt cool, and she joyfully picked it up and climbed down the tree.

Now she held the object in her hand, but was it truly a star? It looked more like a precious, glowing jewel. Istahar peered into it and saw a burning flame, which seemed as if it would never go out. Right in the center of that flame, Istahar thought she saw a face. The closer she looked, the clearer it became. All of a sudden she heard a

voice, the voice of a wise old man. And the voice said:
"Istahar, that is no star in your hand. It is a magic jewel
that has fallen from the Throne of Glory in Paradise,
where God makes His home. Unless that jewel is returned
to its proper place, a great blessing will be lost to the
world."

"But how can I help?" asked Istahar.

"No matter who comes to you—an angel or a
demon—and tries to get you to give up the jewel, don't
give it away. For even the angel will not return it to its
rightful place—angels too can be tempted when they see
something so precious and powerful. Know, Istahar, that
you, and only you, must return that jewel to God's
Throne."

"B-b-but I'm only a little girl. What should I say? And
how will I know if I am faced with an angel or a demon?"
asked Istahar.

"Remember this," said the voice, which really belonged
to the good angel Raziel. "If anyone comes to you who
does not cast a shadow, he is a demon. If he has wings, he
is an angel. To the demon say: 'Demon, tell me, where is
your shadow?' That will take care of him. To the angel
say: 'I won't give you the jewel unless you give me your
wings.' And the minute you have them, fly away with the
jewel. Remember, Istahar, everything depends on you."

All at once the figure in the flame vanished. All Istahar could see was the flame itself, burning as brightly as ever.

She looked up and saw that it had grown very dark, for the moon was covered by a dark cloud. Suddenly Istahar heard a voice saying: "The jewel has grown dark, Istahar. It is useless now. You might as well throw it away."

Istahar looked down and saw that it was true—the flame was almost out. Why, it was no larger than a tiny ember. Istahar shivered with fear and prayed, for if the flame went out, what would protect her?

Then the cloud passed, and the full moon shone brightly again. That is when Istahar saw a dark figure standing in front of the tree—who did not cast a shadow. She knew at once that it must be a demon, trying to steal the precious jewel. And Istahar was no longer afraid. Remembering the words of the old man, she shouted as loud as she could: "Tell me, demon, where is your shadow?"

Instantly the demon vanished. Istahar was alone beneath the moon, and the flame in the jewel burned brightly once more. She breathed a sigh of relief and turned to go, clutching her treasure.

At that moment she saw something bright in the distance, something like a flaming bird. She watched as it came closer, until a radiant being stood in front of her, glowing so brightly that she had to shield her eyes. "Who are you?" she whispered, so afraid that she could hardly speak.

"I have been sent to recover the fallen jewel," said the glowing figure, who had shimmering wings that beat slowly back and forth.

"Are you an angel?" Istahar asked.

"Yes," the angel answered.

And again Istahar remembered the words of the wise man.

"In that case," she said, "there is something you must do for me before I give you the jewel."

"What is it?" asked the angel.

"You must let me try on your wings."

"But that is impossible," said the angel. "My wings do not come off. There is no way I can give them to you."

"I don't believe you," said Istahar, who was clever as well as brave. "If you are an angel, anything should be possible. If you can't give me your wings, you must not be an angel!"

"Of course anything is possible," said the angel. "If you don't believe me, watch...." The angel took off his wings and handed them to Istahar. She put them on right away, and when she felt them beating, she understood how it was possible to fly. All at once she flew off, while the angel looked on, helpless.

[111]

Istahar soared on one long breath into the heavens, and found herself before the Throne of Glory. There she saw nine glowing jewels—exactly like her own—but the place for the tenth jewel was empty. Istahar opened her hand and looked at the precious jewel. Its inner flame burned so brightly and so purely that she felt as if she were invisible in its light. And she carefully put the tenth jewel back in its place in the Throne of Glory.

At that moment the heavens were filled with song, the most beautiful music that Istahar had ever heard. It was the voices of angels, rising up as one, blessing her deed. Above them another voice could be heard, one that seemed to speak from inside her and outside her at the same time. She knew without asking that it was the voice of God. And God said: "Istahar, you have done a great deed. Because of you, the world will be blessed—for I am going to make you the morning star, the brightest in all the sky."

God kissed Istahar, and all at once she found herself glowing as brightly as a sun, filling the darkness with light. On earth everyone looked up and wondered at the new star, which was indeed the brightest in the sky. And all who saw it knew that it was a great blessing.

As for the angel, why, he wandered around the world for many, many years, unable to return to Paradise without his wings. At last God decided that his punishment had lasted long enough and let him find the ladder that Jacob saw in his dream, with angels going up and down its rungs. The angel quickly climbed up the ladder—and that is how the wingless angel finally got back to heaven.

GERMANY: THIRTEENTH CENTURY

SOURCES AND COMMENTARY

THE STUDY of Jewish folklore has been immeasurably assisted by the creation of the Israel Folktale Archives (IFA), under the directorship of Professors Dov Noy of The Hebrew University and Aliza Shenhar of The University of Haifa. We acknowledge with grateful thanks Professors Noy and Shenhar, and Edna Cheichel, curator of the archives, for access to the rich material of the IFA. We would also like to thank Elizabeth Gordon, Leslie Kimmelman, Toni Markiet and Judy Levin, our editors at HarperCollins, for their valuable suggestions and support. Lastly, we wish to gratefully acknowledge the assistance of Arielle North Olson in the editing of these stories.

Each of the tales included has been classified according to the Aarne-Thompson (AT) system, found in *The Types of the Folktale* by Antti Aarne, translated and enlarged by Stith Thompson (Helsinki: 1961). Specific Jewish additions to these types are listed according to the type index of Heda Jason found in *Fabula*, volume 7, pp. 115–224 (Berlin: 1965) and in *Types of Oral Tales in Israel: Part 2* (Jerusalem: 1975). Reference to these tale types will be of use to those seeking both Jewish and non-Jewish variants of the tales included in this collection. All sources are found in Hebrew unless otherwise noted.

[115]

THE GIANT OG AND THE ARK (Palestine)

From *Pirke de Rabbi Eliezer*, Chapter 23. AT 2044.

There are many stories about Og, the biblical giant, found both in the Midrash and in Jewish folklore. The earliest portray him as a fierce enemy of the Jewish people, but in later legends Og is transformed into a well-meaning giant, as in this tale. This story teaches the importance of cooperation.

THE MAGIC PITCHER (Iraq)

Collected by Rachel Khanem from her mother, Regina Bibi. A variant is IFA 4042, collected by Judith Gut from Esther Weinstein. Found in *Savta Esther Messaperet* by Esther Weinstein, edited by Zipporah Kagan. AT 333.

Olive oil was and still is a precious commodity in the Middle East, a fact that is reflected in this story. The miracle of the olive oil echoes the biblical account of Elisha found in II Kings 4:1–7. "The Magic Pitcher" also recalls the journey of the little girl to her grandmother's house in "Little Red Riding Hood" from Grimms' Fairy Tales.

CHUSHAM AND THE WIND (Iraq)

IFA 8534. Told by Moshe Barochof. Another IFA tale about Chusham is IFA 1586, told by Eliyahu Aggasi of Iraq. AT 1690, AT 1696.

The confused but lovable Chusham is the traditional fool of both Middle Eastern (Sephardic) Jewish folklore and its Eastern European counter part (Ashkanazic). This tale teaches children that there is a right way and a wrong way of doing virtually everything.

KATANYA (Turkey)

IFA 8900, written by Moses Gad, told by Sarah Gad. AT 700.

There are more tales about the Prophet Elijah and about King Solomon in Jewish folklore than about any other figures. This one is a typical Elijah tale, where the prophet appears in disguise to help a worthy person in need. "Katanya," which is Hebrew for "God's little one," is a Turkish variant of the Tom Thumb/Thumbelina tale type.

THE MAGIC SANDALS OF ABU KASSIM (Turkey)

IFA 8898, collected by David Gideon from his mother, Sara Gideon. From *Hodesh Hodesh ve-Sippuro 1970*, edited by Dov Noy (Haifa: 1971). AT 745.

Here is another example of an Elijah tale, where a poor man is rewarded for his generosity in sharing his bread with a beggar—who is actually Elijah the Prophet. It is a classic rags-to-riches story.

THE WATER WITCH (The Orient)

From *Alpha Beta de-Ben Sira*, edited by M. Steinschneider (Berlin: 1858). An oral variant is IFA 7248, from *Sippure Am Misanuk*, collected by Samuel Zanvel Pipe, edited by Dov Noy (Haifa: 1967).

The biblical injunction "Cast your bread on the waters, for a time will come when you will find it again" (Ecc. 11:1) is the key to this story about the reward for charity freely given. Leviathan, who is mentioned in the Book of Job, is the Ruler of the Sea in Jewish folklore. The story is a distant variant of "Hansel and Gretel" from Grimms' Fairy Tales.

THE ENORMOUS FROG (Babylon)

From the Babylonian Talmud (Aramaic), tractate Baba Bathra 73b. AT 2031.

The Talmud contains a series of fanciful legends about the travels of Rabbah bar bar Hannah, similar to the kind of tall tales often told by sailors. The enormous frog and the other giant creatures in this tale were some of the amazing sights recounted by Rabbah.

A TALE OF TWO CHICKENS (Babylon)

From the Babylonian Talmud (Aramaic), tractate Ta'anith 25a. AT 2034C.

This is a fable about the virtues of honesty. It is one of many stories told about Rabbi Hanina ben Dosa, a first-century talmudic sage from the Galilee, who was known for his honesty and charity.

A PALACE OF BIRD BEAKS (Yemen)

From *Hadre Teman*, edited by Nissim Binyamin Gamlieli (Tel Aviv: 1978). IFA 11306, collected by Nissim Binyamin Gamlieli from Yehoshua ben Yoseph David. A variant is the Moroccan tale "King Solomon and the Queen Kashira," where the queen agrees to marry Solomon only if he first builds her a palace made entirely of eagles' bones. IFA 1071, collected by Issachar Ben-Ami from Friha Susan. AT *981 (Andrejev).

This is one of many tales about King Solomon, who is portrayed in Jewish folklore as the wisest of men. Here, however, King Solomon learns that even the smallest of creatures have something of value to teach a mighty king. In other stories, the hoopoe bird is identified as King Solomon's favorite messenger and confidant.

THE DIAMOND TREE (Morocco)

IFA 2308. Collected by Yehuda Mazuz from Masuda Mazuz. A variant of "Hansel and Gretel." AT 327.

Like "The Magic Sandals of Abu Kassim," this tale reflects the rags-to-riches fantasy of an impoverished people. The name Nissim means "miracles."

MOVING A MOUNTAIN (Poland)

Collected by Barbara Rush from Chaim Maler (Poland), now a resident of Maskeret Batya, Israel. AT 1326B.

This is one of many humorous folktales about Chelm, a city in Poland that has become identified as a legendary city of fools, where the greatest of the fools are jokingly called sages or "wise men."

[118]

THE BEAR AND THE CHILDREN (Eastern Europe)

From *Yiddisher Folklor* (Yiddish), edited by Yehuda L. Cahan (Vilna: 1931). AT 123.

This is probably the best-known Jewish nursery tale of Eastern Europe— with the exception of the song *"Had Gadya"* ("One Kid"), sung at the end of the Passover seder. The story offers young children the assurance that if there is danger, their parents will do everything possible to save them. It is a variant of "The Wolf and the Seven Kids" from Grimms' Fairy Tales.

THE GOBLIN (Eastern Europe)

From *Tesfunot ve-Aggadot*, Micha Joseph Bin Gorion (Berditchevsky) (Tel Aviv: 1957). AT 307B.

There are many tales of demons in Jewish literature, going back as far as the Talmud, where a seven-headed monster is defeated by a rabbi who pronounces God's name seven times, once for each head (tractate Kiddushim 29b). In Eastern European lore there are many tales about a kind of goblin called a *Lantukh*, which was more annoying than dangerous, like the goblin in our story.

THE PRINCE WHO THOUGHT HE WAS A ROOSTER (Eastern Europe)

From *Maasiyiot U'Meshalim* in *Kochavay Or* (Jersusalem: 1896). A tale of Rabbi Nachman of Bratslav. AT 1543C*.

Rabbi Nachman of Bratslav, one of the greatest Jewish storytellers, commented on this story: "In this way must the genuine teacher go down to the level of his people if he wishes to raise them up to their proper place." This tale can easily be understood by children, who can identify both with the wise man and with the stubborn prince.

THE ANGEL'S WINGS (Germany)

From *Beit ha-Midrash*, edited by Adolf Jellinek, 6 volumes, 2nd ed. (Jerusalem: 1938). A variant is found in *Yalkut Shimoni* (Frankfurt: 1678). An oral variant is found in *Hodesh Hodesh ve-Sippuro 1976–1977*, edited by Dov Noy (Jerusalem: 1979), IFA 10856, collected by Ahuva Baner from Shmuel Nohi of Persian Kurdistan. AT 468, AT 795A* (Andrejev).

This tale is based on the story of the Sons of God and the daughters of men found in Genesis 6. Later rabbinic legends expanded this myth by identifying the "Sons of God" with the angels. In the version of this legend from *Yalkut Shimoni* Istahar escapes the angel by insisting that he reveal the pronounciation of the secret name of God to her before she will yield to him. He does so, and she pronounces it and flies into heaven, where God transforms her into a star.